Princess Milly's Mixed-up Magic

The Ballerina Ball

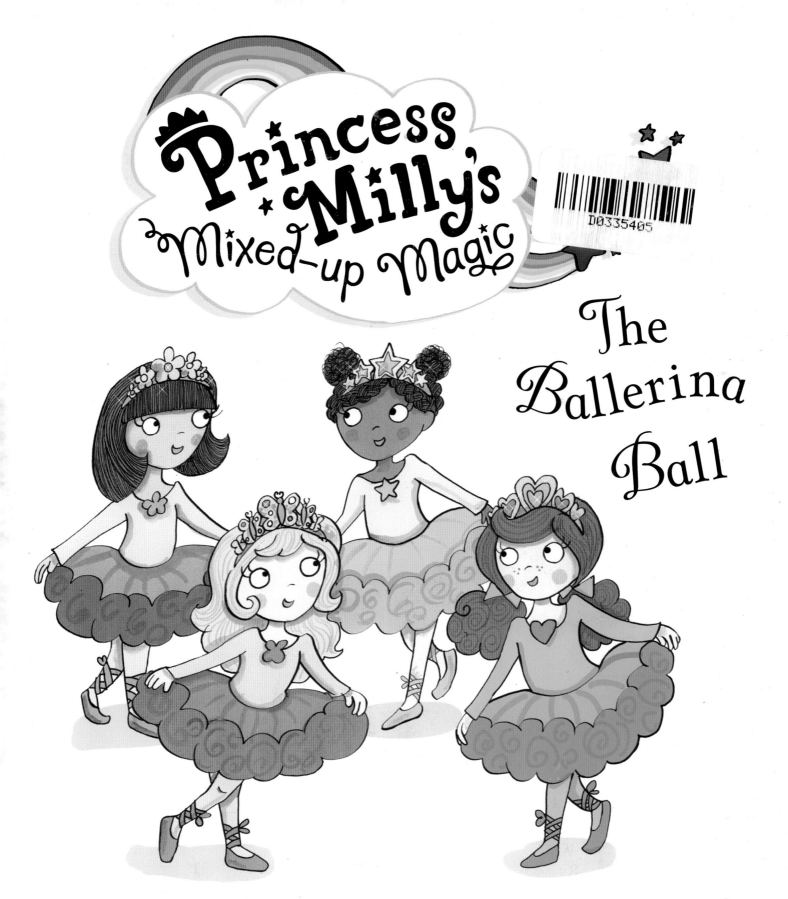

WRITTEN BY Clemency Pearce ✳ ILLUSTRATED BY Lauren Beard

Through the clouds and stars and bits of fluff that float just on the edge of Fairyland stands Rainbow Towers, the most dazzling, magical palace that ever was.

At the tip of the toppest turret lived Princess Milly,
the most magical princess you'll ever meet.

"With a sprinkle of glitter
and a twinkle of fun,

it's time for a party
come on, everyone!"

Princess Milly called to her best friends from her perfectly
pretty balcony. For in the most magical palace that ever was
there lived not just one but four princesses.

There was Princess Bea ...
"A new adventure! Let's go see!
Hurry, Diamond ... What can it be?"

And Princess Ruby ...
"She'll need our help if things
go wrong ... She'll be all
mixed up before too long!"

And, last but not least,
Princess Ella too ...
"Hop and scamper!
Twirl and run! It's time for magic,
games and fun!"

The three princesses hurried to join Milly.
She was super-excited. "Today is the most special day
of the year at Rainbow Towers! It's the Ballerina Ball!"

"YAY!" cheered the princesses.

"Can we wear flowery, floaty frocks?" asked Bea.

"Can we have glittery red shoes?" asked Ruby.

"Can we do our super-special dance routine?" asked Ella.

"We must go to the Star Studio to practise!" said Milly.

So the four princesses whizzed and whooshed

round and down the Secret Spiral Slide

to the special dance studio to get ready!

They whipped on their warm-up leotards

and matching skirts in a flurry of dazzling disco delight.

"Let's practise our routine!" said Milly.
The princesses took their places on the dance floor
and the music began . . .

"Ruby, you're not in time!"
scolded Ella.

"Stop forgetting the steps!"
replied Ruby.

"You need to copy me!"
yelled Bea.

All the princesses were grumbling and squabbling.

"Oh no," said Milly sadly, "this will never do.
We'll never have our routine ready for
the Ballerina Ball at this rate . . ."

"Practice makes perfect, Milly,"
said Sparkle. "Your friends
might need your help."

Then Milly had a brilliant brainwave . . .

"Razzle, dazzle, sparkle and shine. Make my magic work this time!

Magic shoes for princess feet
to make us dance to every beat!"

Spirals and swirls of popping pink dust
exploded around the Star Studio . . .

And suddenly there was tinkling fairy music coming from . . . their shoes!

"My feet are dancing on their own!" called Ella, whirling across the floor.

"I can't stop mine either!" squealed Bea as she flew through the air.

"HELP!" yelled Ruby, who was spinning round and round. "I feel dizzy!"

"Whoops!" said Milly, waltzing past.
"I think I might have magicked our
shoes a bit too much."

"Maybe you should
un-magic them a little?"
suggested Sparkle.

Milly lifted her magic wand once more
as she swooshed around the hall . . .

"Razzle, dazzle, sparkle and shine.

Make my magic work this time!

Swap our naughty, dancing shoes

for graceful partners, soft and smooth!"

"I'm not sure that's a
good idea . . ." said Sparkle,
just a moment too late.

The spell whizzed around the room in a whirlwind of feathery fuzz.

The shoes had gone but the girls were still dancing . . .

this time with **swans!**

"I don't think I want to dance with a giant bird!" grizzled Bea.

"He just pecked my nose!"
cried Ruby.

"And I'm allergic
to feathers!"
sneezed Ella.

It was a very silly sight indeed.

"I've muddled everything up!" sobbed Milly.
"The guests will be arriving soon!
How can we possibly learn the steps in time?"

"Think of your friends, Milly.
If you help them, you'll help yourself too,"
said Sparkle in his wisest voice.

Milly lifted her gleaming pink wand into the air and closed her eyes.

"Razzle, dazzle, sparkle and shine.
Make my magic work this time!
Four ballerinas for the beautiful ball,
the perfect routine is friendship for all!"

The princesses found themselves at the Ballerina Ball. The Ballroom began to fill with guests from all over Fairyland.

"I'm nervous!" whispered Ruby. "Will we get our dance routine right?"

"Don't worry!" said Milly as they took their positions on the dance floor. "You can never go wrong with your best friends around!"

It was **true**.
The princesses . . .

pirouetted,

twirled,

and swayed

. . . perfectly as the crowd clapped and cheered.
It was the most **wonderful dance**
anyone had ever seen!

Soon everyone was having
a fabulous time.

They had their photos taken
for the *Fairyland News* . . .

and danced with the *Pixie Princes* of *Popville*.

The princesses took their final curtsies
as the smiling sun began to set.

"I never thought we'd remember the routine!
I'm so happy everything worked out. It was the most
magical ballerina ball ever!" laughed Ella.

"Working together is always the right step!"
replied Milly, hugging her friends.

Soon the princesses were climbing the stairs to their feather-fluffed beds. As they cuddled up and snuggled down, they whispered their special goodnights.

"Sweet dreams and snuggles, everyone!
See you soon for magic fun!"

As the snoozing moon drifted above the clouds and stars and bits of fluff that float just on the edge of Fairyland, Rainbow Towers – the most dazzling, magical palace that ever was – fell very softly, very quietly, to sleep.

The End

Until next time . . .